Amelia Bedelia
STORYBOOK FAVORITES

by **Herman Parish**

pictures by **Lynne Avril**

Greenwillow Books
An Imprint of HarperCollinsPublishers

Library of Congress Control Number: 2018950765
ISBN 978-0-06-288301-8 (trade ed.)

18 19 20 21 22 SCP 10 9 8 7 6 5 4 3 2 1
Greenwillow Books

✿ Contents ✿

Amelia Bedelia's
First Day of School

1

Amelia Bedelia's
First Field Trip

47

Amelia Bedelia
Makes a Friend   87

Amelia Bedelia
Sleeps Over   123

Amelia Bedelia
Hits the Trail   159

Amelia Bedelia's
·First Day of School·

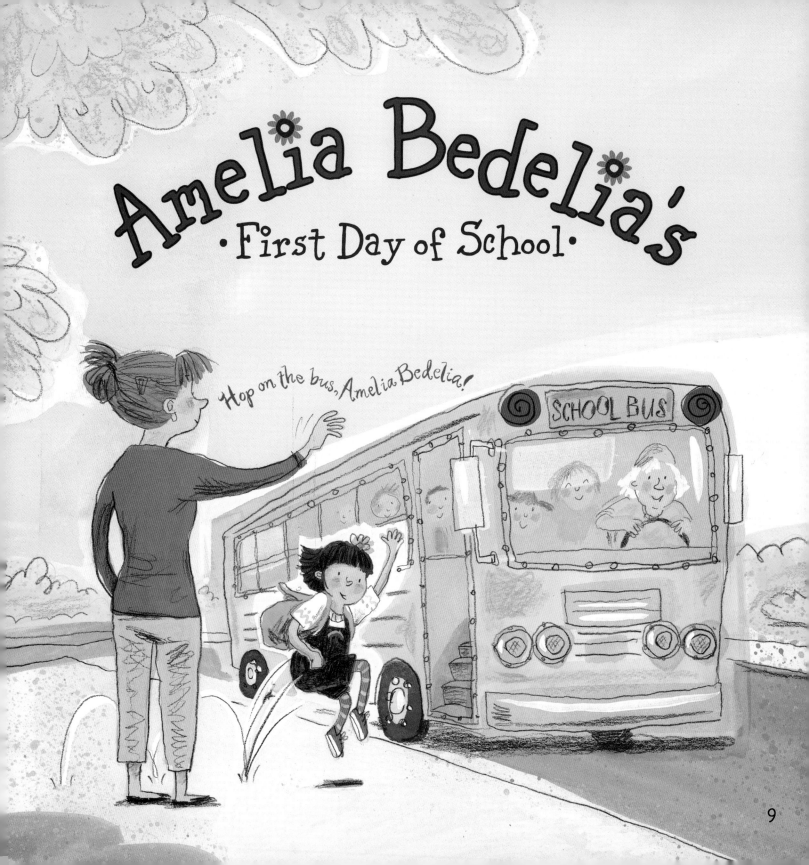

Amelia Bedelia's
•First Day of School•

Hop on the bus, Amelia Bedelia!

SCHOOL BUS

Amelia Bedelia couldn't wait to go to school.
"Here we are," said Mrs. Park, the bus driver. "Time to jump off!"
Amelia Bedelia backed up, then ran as fast as she could,
and jumped as far as she could . . .

Amelia Bedelia landed right on top of a grown-up.

Ooooooof!

"Are you my teacher?" she asked.

"I am Mrs. O'Malley. I teach gym."

"Oh," said Amelia Bedelia. "I am not Jim. I'm Amelia Bedelia.
Can you help me find my teacher?"

"Follow me," said Mrs. O'Malley.

And Amelia Bedelia did . . . right into her new classroom.

"Hello there! My name is Miss Edwards.
 You must be Amelia."
"How did you know?" asked Amelia Bedelia.
"Because you're my last tag," Miss Edwards said.

Amelia Bedelia started running.

"You can't catch me," she yelled. "I'm too fast!"

"Come back!" said Miss Edwards, laughing.

"We aren't playing tag. I have a name tag for you."

15

Amelia Bedelia looked at her name tag.
Something was missing. She added "Bedelia."
"I like my whole name," she said. "It rhymes."
"So it does," said Miss Edwards. "Now please sit
wherever you like."

That was a hard choice for Amelia Bedelia.

She liked the pictures of faraway places.

She liked the letters marching across the top of the board.

She liked the hamster running on its wheel.

She liked everything she saw.
So she sat down right in the middle of the classroom.

17

Miss Edwards began the day by calling the roll.
"Amelia Bedelia?"

"What?" said Amelia Bedelia.

"Not what," said Miss Edwards. "Here."

"I hear you," said Amelia Bedelia.

"Good," said Miss Edwards. "When you hear
your name, say it."

"It!" hollered Amelia Bedelia.

"It?" said Miss Edwards. "Who is it?"

"I will be it!" said Amelia Bedelia. "Can we play tag now?"

Everyone began to laugh.

Clap! Clap! Clap!

"*Shhhhh*. Be as quiet as mice," said Miss Edwards. "Now that I am sure *you* are here, Amelia Bedelia, I'll read the names of your classmates."

"Rose?"
"Here!"

Their names were very exciting, but Amelia Bedelia still loved her name best of all.

Plop! Plop! Plop!

Miss Edwards placed a lump of squishy clay on each desk.
"Let's make our favorite animals," she said.

Amelia Bedelia loved hamsters, so she began making one.

Rose made a giraffe.

Dawn made a pony.

And Clay made a big, fat bullfrog.

"You're funny, Amelia Bedelia," said Clay.
"You could be the teacher's pet."
   Amelia Bedelia was not happy. She loved animals,
but she did not want to be anyone's pet.
She felt like flattening Clay's frog.

"If you have trouble, chickadees," said Miss Edwards,
"try wiggling your fingers on that clay!"

24

So that is exactly what Amelia Bedelia did.
Soon Clay was laughing so hard he could not stop.
"Amelia Bedelia!" said Clay. "Stop tickling me!" 25

"Clean up, clean up, everybody clean up!" sang
Miss Edwards. "It's time for music."
Mrs. Melody arrived with her guitar and tambourine.
"We will sing like birds today, *la-la!*" she trilled.

Then the students toured
the library with Mr. Stacks.
"I want to see your little noses
in the books!" said Mr. Stacks.

OWW!

meow!

In gym class, Mrs. O'Malley
taught them how to run like cheetahs.

At last it was time for lunch.

"Do you feel like a sloppy Joe?" asked the lady behind the lunch counter.

"No!" said Amelia Bedelia. "Do I look like one?"

"Here you are," said the lady. "I hope your eyes aren't bigger than your stomach."

"Me too," said Amelia Bedelia. "They would not fit in my head."

"Amelia Bedelia," said Rose after
lunch. "Do you want to jump rope with us?"
Amelia Bedelia smiled. "Sure!" she said.
She put the rope on the ground and jumped over it.

Amelia Bedelia was a terrific rope jumper.
Rose giggled. So did Holly and Dawn and Joy.
But before long, everyone on the playground
was jumping rope the Amelia Bedelia way!

There was time for one last project. Miss Edwards brought
out big sheets of paper, glue, and scissors.
"This is free time," she said. "Create something wonderful!"

Amelia Bedelia decided to make daisies for her mother.

She got a piece of white paper for the petals.

And a piece of yellow paper for the centers.

And another piece of white paper.

And another piece of yellow paper.

And another piece of white paper.

And another piece of yellow paper.

"Amelia Bedelia," said Miss Edwards. "Don't be a
Ping-Pong ball. Please sit down."
"But . . . but . . . I need green for the stems!"
"Enough is enough," said Miss Edwards. "Please glue
yourself to your seat."

So Amelia Bedelia did. And since her daisies
didn't have stems, she glued them to her headband
until the school day ended.

"Good-bye, squirrels and ladybugs!" said Miss Edwards.
She was standing in the doorway,
giving everyone a gold star.
"See you tomorrow!"
Soon, Amelia Bedelia was the only one left.

"Amelia Bedelia," said Miss Edwards, "why are you still here?"

"Because," said Amelia Bedelia, "you told me to glue myself to my seat."

"So I did," said Miss Edwards.

"And so I did," said Amelia Bedelia.

37

Amelia Bedelia stood up, and the chair stood up with her!
Miss Edwards chuckled, then laughed out loud.
"Oh, Amelia Bedelia," Miss Edwards said. "I should have
known better than to say that to you, especially on
your first day of school."

As Miss Edwards got Amelia Bedelia unstuck,
she whispered, "Want to know a secret?
Today is my first day of school, too.
I am a brand-new teacher."
"We both deserve gold stars,"
said Amelia Bedelia.

"You'll have lots of fun tomorrow,"
said Miss Edwards. "We are
having an assembly."
"Hooray!" said Amelia Bedelia.
"What are we going to build?"

"Memories," said Miss Edwards.
Then she tapped Amelia Bedelia once,
on the very top of her head.
"Tag!" said Miss Edwards. "You are IT until tomorrow."

Amelia Bedelia smiled.
She couldn't wait to come back to school!

Two Ways to Say It!

Amelia Bedelia always takes things literally, and that leads to many funny misunderstandings. Here are a few examples from *Amelia Bedelia's First Day of School*. Can you think of any other words or expressions Amelia Bedelia misunderstands in this story?

Hop on the bus.  Get on the bus.

Her eyes were bigger than her stomach.  The food looked so good she took much more than she could eat.

The teacher's pet.  The student that a teacher likes best.

Amelia Bedelia's nose was in a book.  Amelia Bedelia was reading.

Glue yourself to your chair. 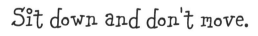 Sit down and don't move.

Meet the Kids in Amelia Bedelia's Class

Amelia Bedelia

The Girls

Angel

Daisy

Holly

Joy

Dawn

Heather

Penny

Rose

The Boys

Chip

Clay

Skip

Teddy

Cliff

Wade

Pat

43

Dressing Amelia Bedelia

Illustrator Lynne Avril designed these clothes for
Amelia Bedelia to wear. Design your own clothes for
Amelia Bedelia—you'll need paper, pencils, paint, or markers.

Amelia Bedelia's
· First Field Trip ·

Amelia Bedelia's
·First Field Trip·

That was a long trip just to see this field!

Amelia Bedelia was so excited about her class field trip to Fairview Farm!

"We learned about farms in school," said Amelia Bedelia's teacher, Miss Edwards. "And today we're on a real farm with real farmers. Say hello to Mr. and Mrs. Dinkins!"

51

"Welcome to Fairview Farm," said Mr. Dinkins.
"I'll take you to see the animals, and then Mrs. Dinkins
will show you her garden. She's got a green thumb.
Now, who wants to meet some chickens?"
"We do!" hollered the whole class.

While everyone followed Mr. Dinkins to the chicken coop, Amelia Bedelia stood very still and looked at Mrs. Dinkins. She had never seen a green thumb before, and she wondered which hand it was on. What colors were the other fingers? Did Mrs. Dinkins have a pink pinky?

53

"Hey, daydreamer!" called Mr. Dinkins.
"Shake a leg!"
Amelia Bedelia looked at her legs.

"Which one?" she asked.
"Which one what?" said Mr. Dinkins.
"You said 'shake a leg,'" said Amelia Bedelia.
"Right," said Mr. Dinkins.

So Amelia Bedelia shook
her right leg and ran to catch up
with her class.

The big rooster perched on top
of the chicken coop was making a racket.
"What a loudmouth!" said Heather
as she covered her ears.
"Roosters don't have mouths,"
said Amelia Bedelia. "He is a loud beak."

Cock·a·doodle·doo!!

"That's Max, and he is our alarm clock," said Mr. Dinkins
as he poured cracked corn into a feeder. "We go to bed
with the chickens and wake up with Max."
Amelia Bedelia was sure glad she didn't have to share
her bed with chickens or a rooster!

55

Mr. Dinkins showed everyone how to gather eggs. Some of the eggs were still warm. There were white eggs and brown eggs and speckled eggs and eggs the color of cream.

"Wow," said Holly. "The eggs match the chickens."

Amelia Bedelia discovered an unusual egg. "Look at this one," she said. "The Easter Bunny must have left it."

"Amelia Bedelia, you crack me up," said Clay.

"Uh-oh," said Amelia Bedelia. "I hope I don't do that to the eggs, too."

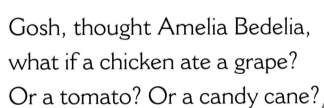

"Is it true," asked Miss Edwards, "that if a chicken eats something green, like broccoli, she'll lay a green egg?"

Gosh, thought Amelia Bedelia, what if a chicken ate a grape? Or a tomato? Or a candy cane?

"Actually," said Mr. Dinkins, "the color of the eggshell depends on the type of chicken. What they eat makes the yolk lighter or darker. Our hens eat good things, so their yolks are bright yellow like the sun."

The next stop was the dairy barn.

"This is Sunshine, my favorite cow," said Mr. Dinkins.

58   "Who'd like to milk her?"

MEOW!!

Everyone took a turn milking Sunshine. It was tricky work!

"Nice shot, Wade!" said Teddy, laughing.

"Mooooooo!" said Sunshine.

"We have twenty dairy cows, four horses, a herd of goats, and a litter of pigs," said Mr. Dinkins, as he led the class on a tour of the barnyard.

"Look," said Amelia Bedelia. "That baby horse has a ponytail, just like Rose!"

"A baby horse is called a foal," said Miss Edwards. "She's still learning to walk."

"Miss Edwards," said Mr. Dinkins, pointing at the baby goats. "Do your kids ever act like *these* kids?"

"They sure do," said Miss Edwards. "But only at recess."

"Here's our litter," said Mr. Dinkins. Amelia Bedelia didn't see any trash—just ten piglets eating. "Those little piggies went to lunch," said Penny. "So should we," said Mr. Dinkins.

61

Mrs. Dinkins was waiting for them under an enormous oak tree. She gave each student a chore to do, and soon everyone was helping to get lunch ready.

Angel, Teddy, and Clay wiped down the picnic tables.

Cliff, Daisy, and Dawn swept off the benches.

Wade, Rose, and Heather folded napkins.

Holly, Joy, and Penny filled
the water glasses.

Chip, Skip, and Pat
passed out cheese and bread.

"Hmmm," said Miss Edwards. "Where is Amelia Bedelia?"

"I asked her
to toss the salad,"
said Mrs. Dinkins.
"Oh dear,"
said Miss Edwards.

63

By the time Miss Edwards found Amelia Bedelia, the salad bowl was empty. "Where did you toss the salad?" asked Miss Edwards.

"I tossed it all over," said Amelia Bedelia.

"Over there.

And over there

and there

and there."

65

After everyone had worked together to make a new salad, the class had lunch. Then Mr. and Mrs. Dinkins took them to the hay barn. They each got to sit on a real tractor. And they lined up to take turns on the rope swing.

Guess who was brave enough to go first?

"Hey, look out!" said Holly.

"Look out, hay!" shouted Amelia Bedelia, landing in a big, bouncy pile.

Mr. Dinkins yawned. "I'd like to hit the hay, too," he said.
"Have a quick nap, dear," said Mrs. Dinkins. "We'll go to the garden."

On the way to the garden, Mrs. Dinkins told the class that potatoes sprout eyes, corn has ears, and lettuce grows a head. Her vegetables came to life for Amelia Bedelia.

ShussQuonch!

"What was that?" Chip asked.

Mrs. Dinkins looked at what he had stepped on by mistake.

"That's a squash," she said.

"It is now," said Amelia Bedelia.

"It is totally squashed."

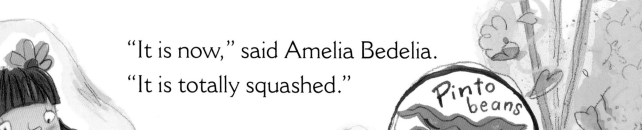

Pinto beans

Navy beans

Wax beans

Rattlesnake beans

Butter beans

While Chip cleaned his shoe, Mrs. Dinkins talked about plants. "We make sure they get plenty of water and sunshine," she said. "This year I planted all sorts of beans—string beans, lima beans, wax beans, scarlet runner beans, soybeans. . . ."

Amelia Bedelia raised her hand. "Do you grow jelly beans?" she asked.

"Well," said Mrs. Dinkins, laughing, "I've never tried to grow a jelly bean, but I'll show you how jelly grows. Follow me."

11

"Welcome to my berry patch," said Mrs. Dinkins. "Help yourself!
I pick the berries and cook them down for jams and jellies."

As Amelia Bedelia reached for a raspberry, she got snagged on thorns.
When Mrs. Dinkins untangled her, Amelia Bedelia saw her thumbs.
"Mrs. Dinkins," she said, "your thumbs aren't one bit green!"
Mrs. Dinkins smiled. "If you're good at growing things, folks say you
have a green thumb. But you've got to get your hands dirty first."

Getting dirty sounded like great fun to Amelia Bedelia.
"Here, try these blueberries," said Mrs. Dinkins. "But only pick
the blue ones. If a blueberry is red, then it is green. Unripe berries
can give you a tummyache."
How can a berry be blue, red, and green at the same time?
Amelia Bedelia wondered.

"Thank you," she said. "But I prefer
strawberries. When they are red,
they're great!"

73

It was a long and exciting day at Fairview Farm, but finally it was time to say good-bye.

"Will the bus be here soon?" asked Amelia Bedelia.

"Actually," said Miss Edwards, "we'll be picked up in car pools."

"Goody," said Amelia Bedelia. "I could use a swim."

"We're mighty glad you came to visit," said Mr. Dinkins. "We have surprise souvenirs for each one of you."

Mrs. Dinkins held out a handful of seeds. "Plant these," she said. "Water them well and give them lots of sunlight. Then one day you'll have pumpkins."

"Pumpkins!" the class yelled. "Hooray for Fairview Farm!"

The next day, Amelia Bedelia's class drew pictures for Mr. and Mrs. Dinkins. Miss Edwards wrote a thank you note and they all signed it. Then they got busy planting their pumpkin seeds.

Everyone got a seed and a cup filled with soil.

"How deep should we plant it?" asked Joy.

"This deep," said Amelia Bedelia, plunging her thumb into the dirt.

She dropped her seed in the hole she'd made and covered it up.

The rest of the class did the same.

"Look," said Amelia Bedelia. "I've got a brown thumb!"

"That's a start," said Miss Edwards. "I'm sure it will turn green in no time!"

And it certainly did.

Spot the Difference

These two pictures are not exactly the same. Five things from picture #1 are missing from picture #2. Can you spot them?

#1

FAIRVIEW FARM
555 FARM MARKET RD.

MEOW!!

#2

FAIRVIEW FARM
555 FARM MARKET RD.

Two Ways to Say It!

Amelia Bedelia always takes things literally, and that leads to many funny misunderstandings. Here are a few examples from *Amelia Bedelia's First Field Trip*. Can you think of any other words or expressions Amelia Bedelia misunderstands in this story?

You crack me up!  You are making me laugh.

Shake a leg, Amelia Bedelia. Hurry up, Amelia Bedelia!

Mrs. Dinkins has a green thumb. Mrs. Dinkins is very good at growing plants.

Please toss the salad.  Please mix up the salad ingredients so the salad is ready to eat.

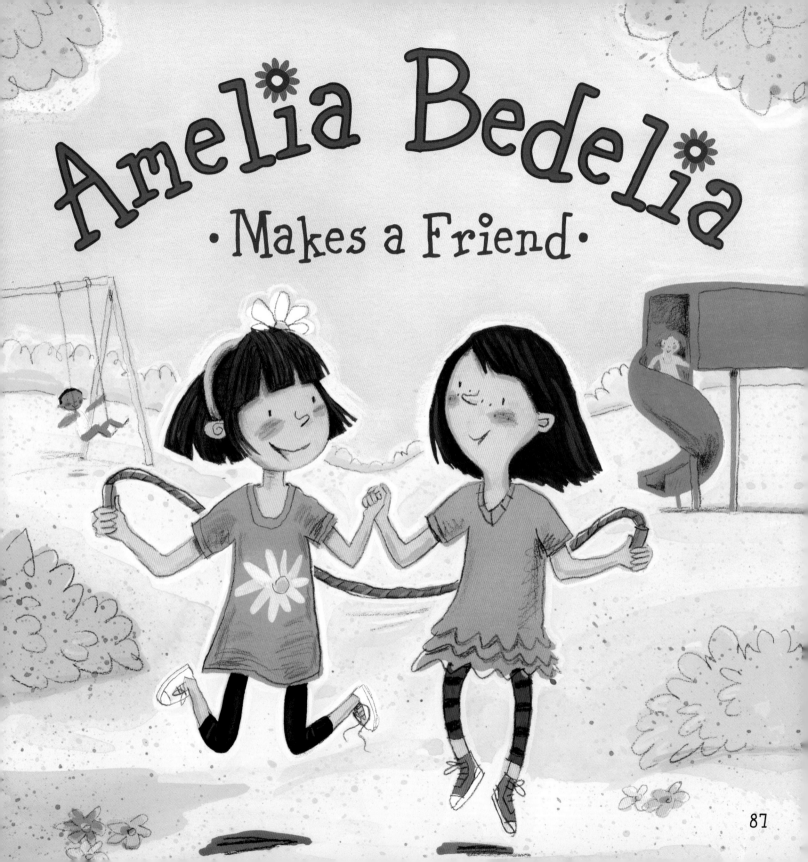

Amelia Bedelia

• Makes a Friend •

Amelia Bedelia was lucky.

Her best friend lived next door.

"Hello, Jen!" said Amelia Bedelia.

"Hi, Amelia Bedelia!" said Jen.

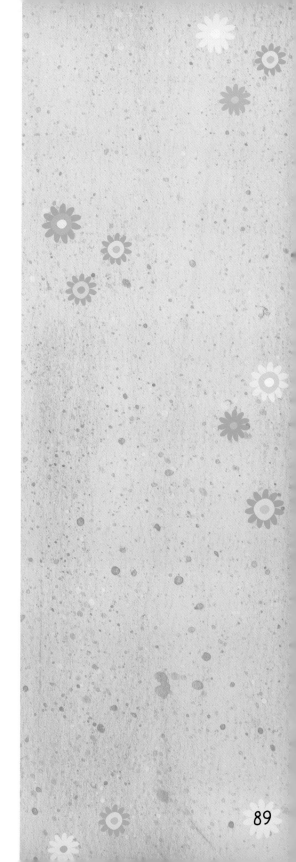

Amelia Bedelia and Jen

had been friends

since they were babies.

They baked together.

They dressed up together.

They played music together.

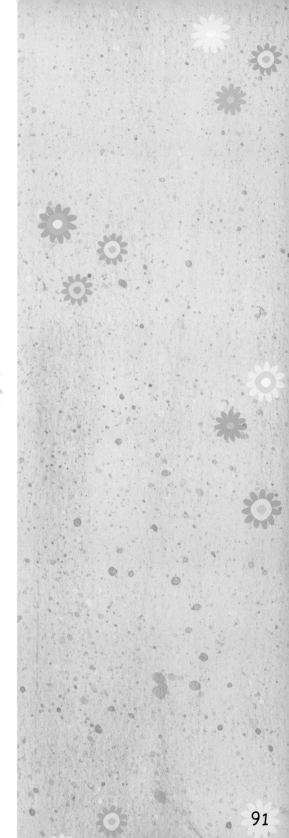

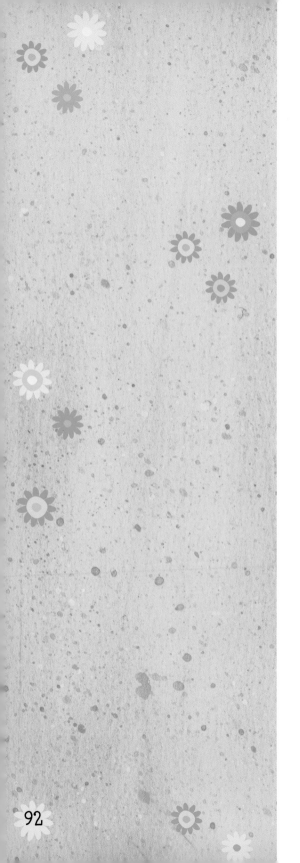

Amelia Bedelia even showed Jen
how to bowl.

"They play so well together,"
said Amelia Bedelia's mother.

"They sure do," said Jen's mother.

"Even though they are
as different as night and day."

Then one day,

Jen and her parents

moved away.

Amelia Bedelia and her parents

were very sad.

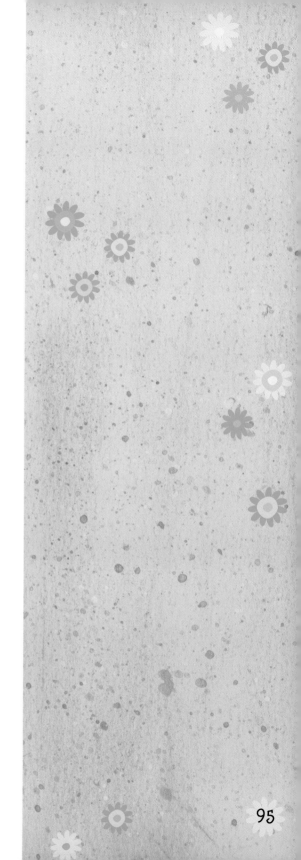

Amelia Bedelia missed Jen.

She missed Jen every day.

She wished Jen would come back.

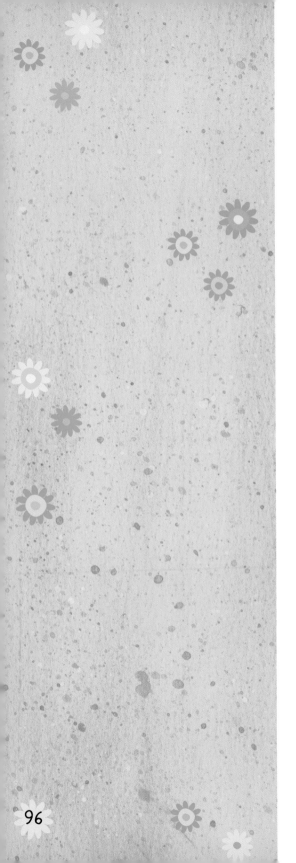

One morning, a moving van pulled up.

"Did Jen come back?"

asked Amelia Bedelia.

"I don't think so,"

said Amelia Bedelia's mother.

"We must have new neighbors."

Amelia Bedelia's mother
watched the movers.
"Oh, look," she said.
"I see a fancy footstool."

Amelia Bedelia did not look.
She wanted Jen back.

"Look!" said Amelia Bedelia's mother.

"I see a coffee table."

Amelia Bedelia still did not look.

She just kept drawing.

Amelia Bedelia's
mother said,
"I see some
big armchairs."

"I see a loveseat."

"I see a twin bed."

Finally, Amelia Bedelia looked
at Jen's old house.

Then she looked at her drawings.

"Our new neighbors sound strange,"
she said.

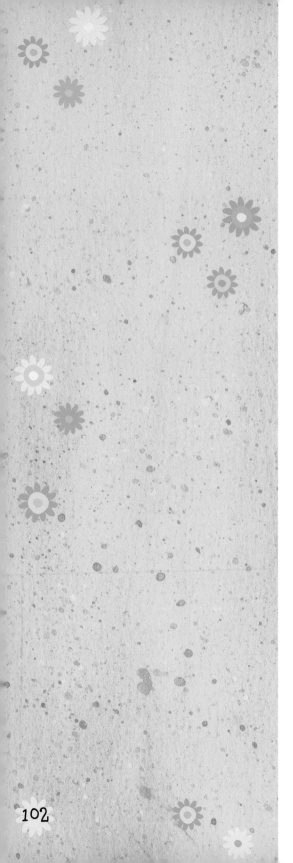

That night, Amelia Bedelia
told her dad
about the new neighbors.

He loved her pictures.

"Amazing!" her dad said.

"I hope they have a pool table."

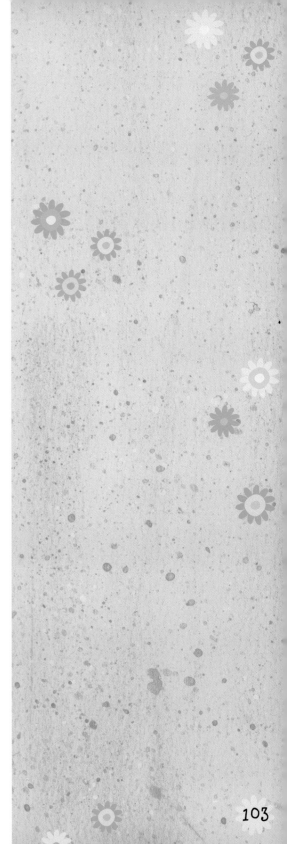

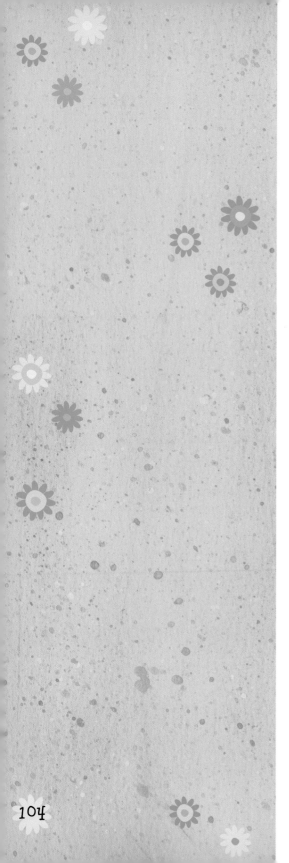

The next morning,
Amelia Bedelia and her mother
baked blueberry muffins.

They took the muffins
next door.

A lady opened the door.

"Hello there," she said.

"My name is Mrs. Adams.

You must be my new neighbors."

"No," said Amelia Bedelia.

"We already live here.

You are my new neighbor."

"You know," said Mrs. Adams,

"I think both of us are right.

Do come in."

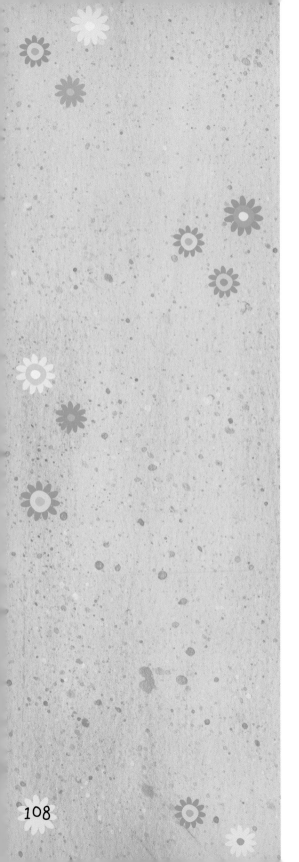

"Mmmm," Mrs. Adams said.

"What smells so good?"

"My mom does," said Amelia Bedelia.

"I don't wear perfume yet."

Jen's house looked different.

Every room was full of boxes.

"Welcome to my mess,"

said Mrs. Adams.

"I will live out of boxes for a while."

That sounded fun to Amelia Bedelia.

"Are the twins in their bed?"

asked Amelia Bedelia.

"My goodness," said Mrs. Adams.

"You have sharp eyes."

Amelia Bedelia hoped that was good.

"My twin grandchildren
will visit today," said Mrs. Adams.
"Their names are Mary and Marty."

The twins visited that afternoon.

"Our grandma is a lot of fun,"

they told Amelia Bedelia.

They were right!

It was great to have a friend

right next door again.

Amelia Bedelia and Mrs. Adams
baked together.

They dressed up together.

They played music together.

113

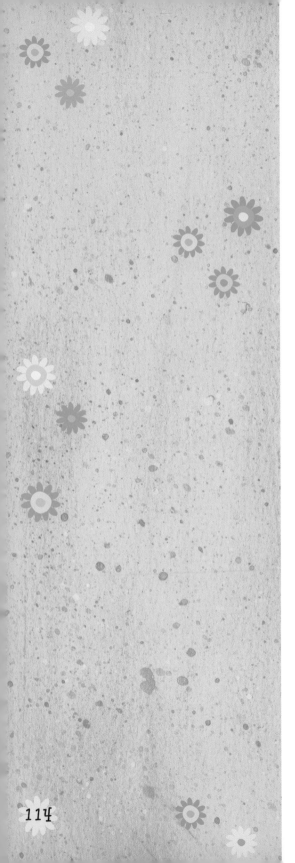

"They have so much fun together,"
said Amelia Bedelia's father.
"They sure do,"
said Amelia Bedelia's mother.
"Even though they are
as different as night and day."

One day Jen came back to visit.

Mrs. Adams took both girls

to a real bowling alley.

"This is the best day ever,"

said Amelia Bedelia.

"I have a best old friend

and a best new friend.

We are three best friends together!"

Two Ways to Say It!

Amelia Bedelia always takes things literally, and that leads to funny misunderstandings. Here are some confusing expressions from *Amelia Bedelia Makes a Friend*. Can you think of any other words or expressions Amelia Bedelia misunderstands in this story?

As different as night and day.

Completely different in every way.

Living out of boxes.

Using things before all the boxes are unpacked.

You have sharp eyes.

You see and notice everything.

Spot the Difference

These two pictures are not exactly the same. Five things from picture #1 are missing from picture #2. Can you spot them?

#1

#2

Missing things: heart on chair, drawing on paper, thought bubble over Dad's head, rubber duck, pink stripe on umbrella

Amelia Bedelia's Mixed-up Words

Amelia Bedelia is all mixed up! Help her by unscrambling these words.
(Hint: Use the pictures to help you figure out the words.)

W I G N S

_ _ _ _ _

U S M I C

_ _ _ _ _

N D I F R E S

_ _ _ _ _ _ _

E K A B

_ _ _ _

Amelia Bedelia
·Sleeps Over·

Amelia Bedelia was excited.

Tonight was her very first sleepover.

All the girls in her class

were going to Rose's house

for a slumber party.

Amelia Bedelia and her mother

drove to Rose's house.

"Is a slumber party fun?"

asked Amelia Bedelia.

"Because sleeping is boring."

"You might not sleep much,"

said her mother.

"You will play, eat pizza, paint nails . . ."

"Do we paint the nails
and then hammer them?"
asked Amelia Bedelia.

"Or do we hammer them first?"

Amelia Bedelia's mother laughed.

"You'll have fun, sweetie," she said.

"I promise."

When Amelia Bedelia arrived,

the front door swung open.

Her friends ran out to greet her.

Rose's mother came outside, too.

129

"Good luck," said Amelia Bedelia's mom.

"I think I'll need it!" said Rose's mother.

"I am a light sleeper."

"Me too," said Amelia Bedelia.

She reached into her backpack

and pulled out her flashlight.

"I sleep with this light every night."

The girls played board games.

Amelia Bedelia had worried

that she would be bored,

but she was not.

Next, everyone went outside
and played tag
until the sun began to set.

"The pizza is here!"
called Rose's father.
"Come and get it!"

"And for dessert," said Rose's mother,

"we will toast marshmallows

and make s'mores."

"Won't that wreck your toaster?"
asked Amelia Bedelia.

"Marshmallows melt into gooey, blobby . . ."

Rose's father laughed.

"We'll toast them on the grill," he said.

After the pizza was gone,

Dawn speared a marshmallow

on Amelia Bedelia's stick.

Holly showed her how to turn it

carefully and slowly

to get a crunchy brown skin.

Amelia Bedelia put her marshmallow

on top of a chocolate bar

between two graham crackers.

"Yum!" said Amelia Bedelia.

"I'd like some more, please!"

"Now you know why

they're called s'mores!" said Rose.

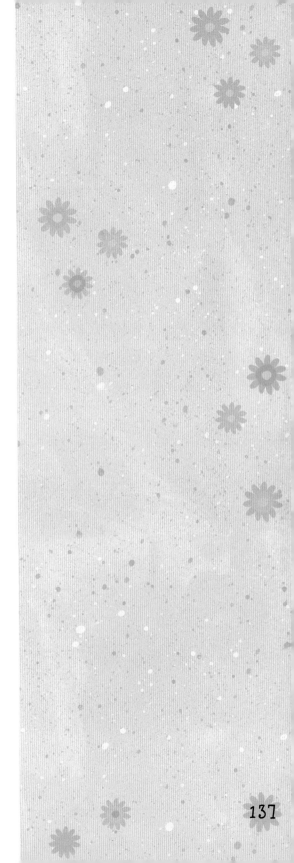

After many more s'mores,

the girls went inside the house.

They put on their pajamas,

but it was not time to slumber yet.

Rose brought out bottles

of glittery nail polish

in more colors than the rainbow.

Every color had the perfect name.

Heather painted

Amelia Bedelia's nails

with

"Shamrock Green"

on her left hand,

"Blue Iceberg"
on her right hand,

and

"Banana Sunrise"

on her right foot.

She saved her left foot for "Cotton Candy Cupcake."

Amelia Bedelia sighed and said,
"I'm so happy
we don't have to hammer them!"

Too soon, the clock struck ten.

"Bedtime, girls!" said Rose's mother.

"Lights out, and no giggling allowed!"

Oh well, thought Amelia Bedelia.

Here comes the slumber part

of this slumber party.

Off went the lights and lamps.

On went Amelia Bedelia's flashlight.

She showed her friends how to make

shadow puppets on the wall.

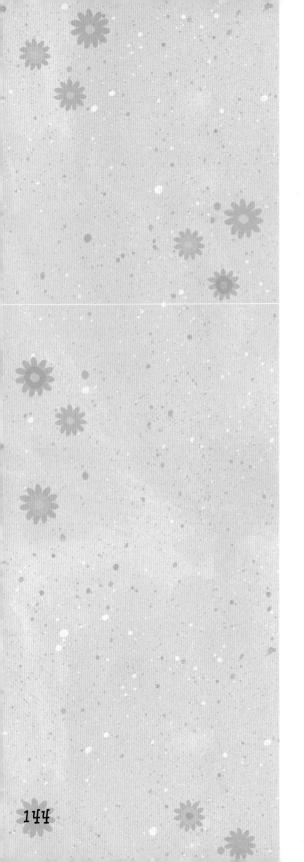

One by one,

the girls fell asleep.

All except Amelia Bedelia.

She was not one bit sleepy.

She made a rabbit.

Then a barking dog.

Then an elephant

with a trunk to grab . . .

Oops!

Her flashlight went out.

"Oh, no," said Amelia Bedelia.

What light would keep her company now?

Then Amelia Bedelia noticed

a very bright light

peeking into the family room.

She pulled back the curtains.

A full moon shone down on her.

Now there was too much light!

Amelia Bedelia dragged her sleeping bag
under Rose's Ping-Pong table.

Perfect, thought Amelia Bedelia.
Now I am having a sleepover
and a sleep under.

Amelia Bedelia snuggled down
into her cozy sleeping bag.
She gazed up at the moon.
She had heard people say that
there was a man in the moon.
She'd never seen him, until tonight.

He looked just like her dad.

Amelia Bedelia closed her eyes.

A second later, she was sound asleep.

The next morning,

the girls had a pillow fight.

Then they made chocolate chip pancakes

and helped to clean up the mess.

Amelia Bedelia's dad picked her up.

"Nice nails," said her father.

"Thanks, moon man," said Amelia Bedelia.

"Huh?" said her father.

"You sound like you need to take a nap."

And so Amelia Bedelia did,

all the way home.

Spot the Difference

These two pictures are not exactly the same. Five things from picture #1 are missing from picture #2. Can you spot them?

#1

#2

Missing things: star on Amelia Bedelia's shirt, piece of popcorn on table, picture on the wall, nail polish bottle on tray, collar on Penny's shirt

Party Planner

Amelia Bedelia did all of these fun things at her first sleepover. What would *you* do at your sleepover?

Play fun games

Eat pizza

Toast marshmallows and make s'mores

Polish fingernails and toenails

Eat popcorn

Make shadow puppets

Have a pillow fight

Eat pancakes

Go home. Yay, sleepovers!

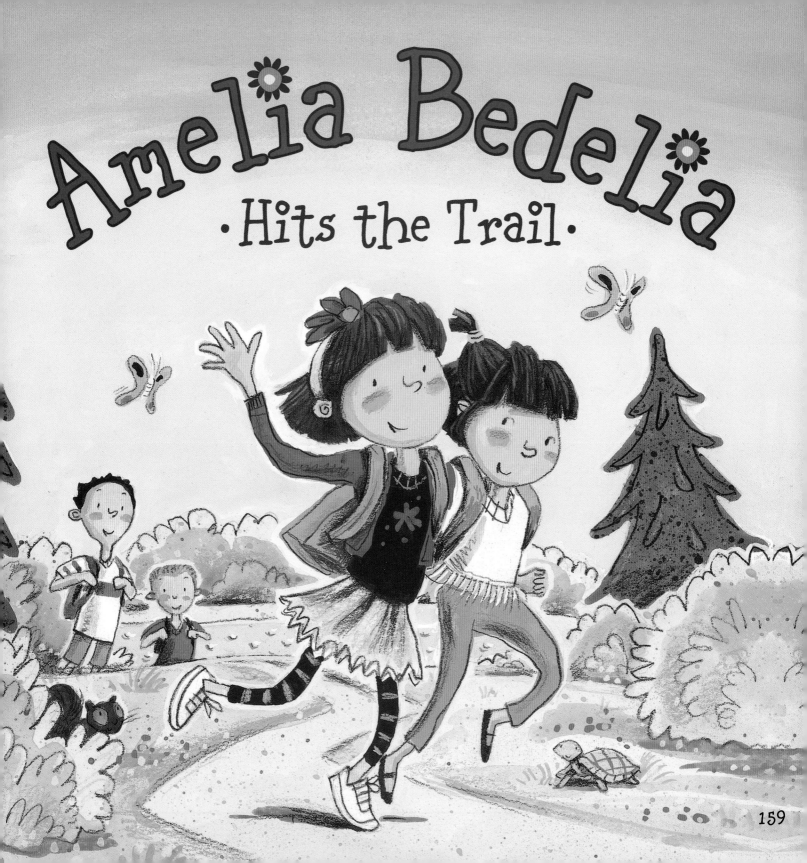

Amelia Bedelia

•Hits the Trail•

Amelia Bedelia was going hiking.

Her entire class was going, too.

"Let's hit the trail," said Miss Edwards,

Amelia Bedelia's teacher.

The trail was steep.

 Everyone stepped over a big tree root.

Amelia Bedelia was chatting

and looking up at the birds and . . .

SPLAT!!

Amelia Bedelia fell flat on her face.

"Are you okay?" asked Miss Edwards.

"I'm okay," said Amelia Bedelia.

"But the next time I hit the trail,

I'll use this stick instead of my face!"

Amelia Bedelia and her friends
spotted lots of living things
along the trail.

They saw a deer
and a rabbit.

They saw squirrels
and chipmunks.

They saw insects
crawling along the ground

and flying in the air.

Birds chirped
in the trees.

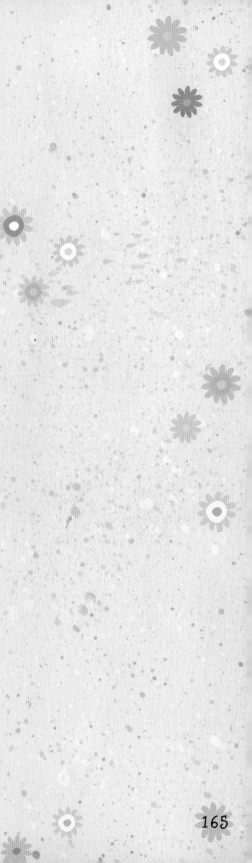

When a snake crossed the trail,
Chip let out a yell.

"Relax," said Penny.
"It is more scared of you
than you are of it."

The class walked slowly.

"Let's move a little faster,"
said Miss Edwards.

"Pick up your snail's pace."

Amelia Bedelia looked for a snail

with a pace to pick up.

Maybe she could find one

for the classroom nature table.

"I'm hungry," said Clay.

"Can we eat lunch?"

Miss Edwards read her map.

"There is a stream ahead," she said.

"We can stop there for a bite."

"I have lots of bites," said Amelia Bedelia.

"I can see water!" said Penny.

The class raced to the stream.

"We'll eat lunch on the bank.

Dig in!" said Miss Edwards.

Amelia Bedelia
didn't see a bank,

or even a cash machine.

Was there treasure buried here?

Why else would Miss Edwards tell them

to dig in?

It was time to go back to school.

Wade was the last to finish his lunch.

"Let's go, Wade," said Miss Edwards.

"Yay!" said Amelia Bedelia.

Amelia Bedelia took off

her shoes and socks

and waded right into the stream.

Soon everyone was splashing

with Amelia Bedelia.

Even Miss Edwards joined the fun.

As they walked back,
everyone found things
for the nature table.

Daisy picked a daisy.

Holly plucked
a sprig of holly.

Rose found
a wild rose.

Amelia Bedelia

picked up fallen leaves.

"What did you find, Amelia Bedelia?"

asked Miss Edwards.

"These are my leafs," said Amelia Bedelia.

Miss Edwards smiled.

"When you have more than one leaf,

you say *leaves*," she said.

That made sense to Amelia Bedelia.

In the fall, every leaf

had to leave its tree.

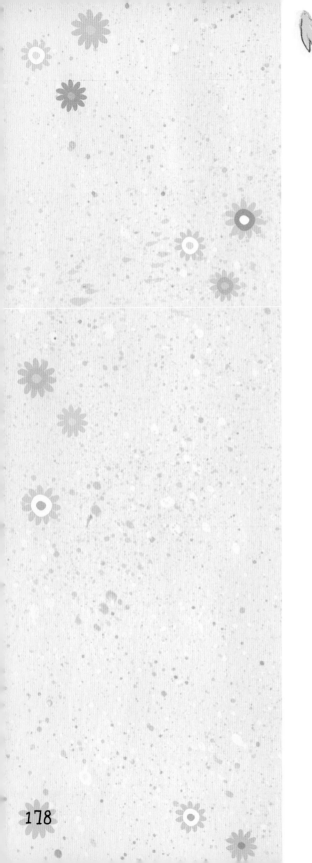

Amelia Bedelia knew

she would not think anymore

of a leaf falling off a tree.

She would think

it was leaving

its tree.

"Nice leaves," said Skip.

"You have maple,

oak,

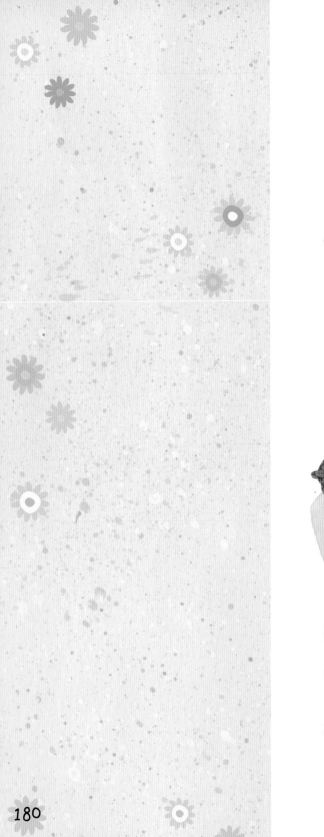

and chestnut," he said.

Skip knew a lot about trees.

"What is this red one?"

asked Amelia Bedelia.

"Uh-oh," said Skip. "That is poison ivy!"

YEE-AHHHH!!!

Amelia Bedelia threw the leaves

up in the air.

Her leaves were leaving again!

Skip laughed so hard

he fell on the ground.

"I was joking!" he said.

Amelia Bedelia was not laughing.

"That was a mean trick," she said.

"Maybe you should take a hike,"
said Skip.

"I am," said Amelia Bedelia.

"And now I don't have anything
for the nature table."

Amelia Bedelia's lip trembled.

"I'm sorry, Amelia Bedelia," said Skip.

He helped Amelia Bedelia

pick up her leaves.

"Hold still!" Skip said.

"Are you teasing again?"

asked Amelia Bedelia.

"No. You have a hitchhiker," said Skip.

He pointed at a caterpillar.

The caterpillar was crawling

on Amelia Bedelia's backpack.

"Wow!" said Amelia Bedelia.

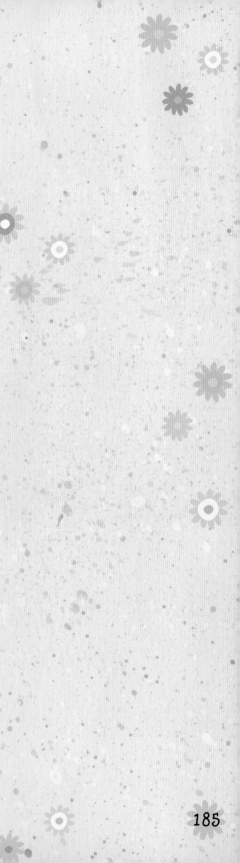

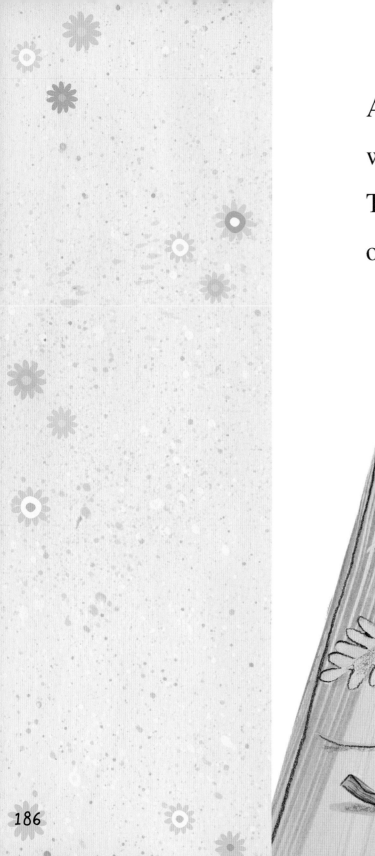

Amelia Bedelia's caterpillar

was the star of the nature table.

Then it was the star

of Amelia Bedelia's classroom . . .

NATURE TABLE

Things WE FOUND
on OUR HIKE!!

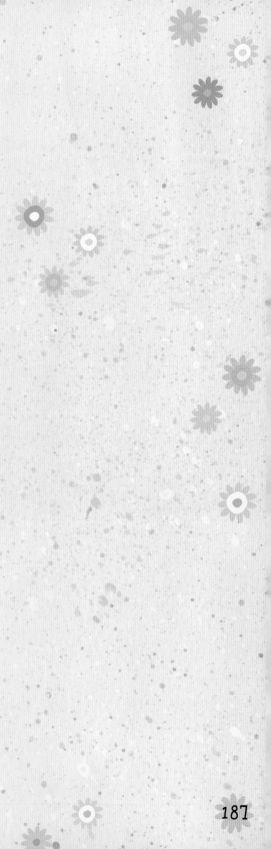

until it hit the trail.

Two Ways to Say It!

Amelia Bedelia always takes things literally, and that leads to many funny misunderstandings. Here are a few examples from *Amelia Bedelia Hits the Trail*. Can you think of any other words or expressions Amelia Bedelia misunderstands in this story?

Let's hit the trail!  Let's get going.

Moving at a snail's pace. Moving super slowly.

Dig in! Start eating.

Take a hike! Go away!

More books about Amelia Bedelia

Amelia Bedelia's First Valentine
BY HERMAN PARISH · PICTURES BY LYNNE AVRIL

Amelia Bedelia's First Apple Pie
BY HERMAN PARISH · PICTURES BY LYNNE AVRIL

Amelia Bedelia's First Vote
BY HERMAN PARISH · PICTURES BY LYNNE AVRIL

Amelia Bedelia's First Library Card
BY HERMAN PARISH · PICTURES BY LYNNE AVRIL

I Can Read! 1
Amelia Bedelia Tries Her Luck
by Herman Parish · pictures by Lynne Avril

I Can Read! 1
Amelia Bedelia Joins the Club
by Herman Parish · pictures by Lynne Avril

Amelia Bedelia Means Business
by Herman Parish · pictures by Lynne Avril

Amelia Bedelia Unleashed
by Herman Parish · pictures by Lynne Avril

Amelia Bedelia Road Trip!
by Herman Parish · pictures by Lynne Avril

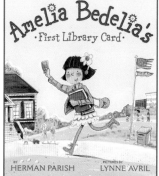